THE ADVENTURE RUN

SOUMY MITTAL

ISBN 979-888569068-3

Contents

1. The Mystery Of Cristiano Zen 1

2. The Frost Walker Man 8

3. The Time Wars 18

4. The Detective Engineer 31

5. The Self Made Girl 33

CHAPTER ONE

The Mystery of Cristiano Zen

Once upon a time in a small village, there lived a guy named Steve with his small family. Steve was a brave guy who work all day for his family. His parent's name was Max and Jenny and he also has a sister named Oliver.

20 years back his father was at his work and they live in a different village. Steve was at his home with Oliver and his two brothers, Suddenly a guy named Cristiano Zen came into that village with his guards and enter Max's house and ask for rent of 6 months. All the children feared out. Then Cristiano Zen buried the whole village.

Steve's both brothers died and after that, no one saw Cristiano and her "The Mystery Of Cristiano Zen" begins:

Chapter-1
Preparation

After then Steve decided to takc revenge for his brother's death. He went on a long journey to find Zen. Steve was just 15 years old so he can't do anything very tough so he decided to do a very strong preparation. After listening to the news of his children's death and the destruction of the village, he got a heart attack "God save him" but his entire body got paralyzed. So Steve was the last hope for his whole family, So Steve decided to do a job of farming.

Steve lost all the hope for the revenge of his brother's death, suddenly a guy came to him and said "I knew what happened to your family" here is the location for the castle of Zen and go take your revenge" then Steve said "How? How! How do you know that?" that guy said, "He is my enemy before you but you we need a strong preparation" then Steve decided to prepare himself for the fight and made himself strong enough. Then that guy also joined him and his name was Jack.

Chapter-2

The Beginning Of the journey

After that Steve and Jack started their journey and then Steve followed Jack to go to Zen's castle. They were going there very wrathfully on that day and don't get into any trouble.

(At Night)

They were going from a cave but then they get a strange person then...

Steve - "What, What's that? Is it a mob or something? Tell me?"

Jack - "No, It's not that, we are getting close to his castle, that's why these dangerous mobs are getting here. When we get more close, we get too many mobs that are more hazardous than these."

Steve - "But tell me what was that? Is it a zombie or something else?"

Jack - "Yes you are right it is a zombie and when you get more close there is more. There are four stages. Here's the list:-

1st stage- Zombie

2nd stage- Skeleton
3rd stage- Spider
4th stage- ???(unknown)

Steve - "Who is the fourth?

Jack - "I also don't know what's the fourth??? But I know a bit little that it's something very immense and very hazardous. Everybody says him unknown...

Steve - " Ok, Let's go there and fight with him.

Jack - " Yes, Let's go.

(Then they fight with them and get to the 3rd stage where Steve get injured a little bit)

(Then they get more close to the castle and get to the 4th stage)

(They get more afraid that what's fourth???)

Steve - "Hey we get to the fourth one but nothing is there"

(Then an explosion takes place there)

Steve - "Oh no!! What is this?? Making explosions everywhere, and flying everywhere. I can't catch it."

Jack - " It's wither! It makes explosion everywhere and damages us very hard. It is impossible to fight and win from him."

Steve - "Nothing is impossible for me. I can fight with him and win from him, Let's fight, Goo!!!"

(Then they fight with him but cannot defeat him then)

Jack - "We can't defeat him it is impossible!!

It is very strong."

Steve - "I have an idea. See you go from the right and I will from the left. Take his head point he has his power in his head buckle. We both at a time attack him and swash his buckle. Mission Swashbuckle. Go.

Jack - "Yes, Go."

(Then they attacked together at his buckle and defeated him)

Jack - “You are brilliant. You can defeat anyone. I think you also defeat Zen. Hope it becomes true.”

Steve - “Yup, now let’s go ahead in the castle.”

Jack - “Yes”

Steve - “Hey jack see there wow what a castle. It’s beautiful but so dangerous to see there, there is a mob at every gate. The gateways were also so huge. How he made this?”

Jack - “He doesn’t made this. The people he kidnapped made this. Because Zen frightened them and forced them to make this. It is made by hundreds of laborers. In this, my father was also encompassed.”

Steve - “Are you serious? How egotistic and grasping he is.”

Jack - “Yes, Let’s go in there. Make yourself ready to go in and also to bout.”

Steve - “I am ready, every time.”

(After that in between they get to slip into a cave where they get a man carrying very different and strange things)

Steve - “Who are you? Are you also with Zen?

The Man - “No, I am here to help you. Take this dragon sword which helps you to kill Zen but not try to use it twice because it can be used only once. You have to search for his weak point and aim there. This will kill him in one shot. Trust me. But don’t use it twice or on his slaves. Ok, now you go there.

Steve - “ We will always be thankful to you. Bye, we are leaving now. Let’s go jack.”

(Then they are going there, And started fighting)

(But after that they can’t fight because they are in no. of 1000 or more)

Jack - "They are so many, We can't fight like this, Let's go back and then come with a strategy"

Steve - "Yes you are right, Let's go"

Jack - "Thank God, We came back, Now tell me what's the plan, If you know."

Steve - "Yes, I know but it is a little bit challenging because they know that we are coming here and I make sure that they tell Zen also." Now listen to my plan, We go there from that upside building, and with these gumboots, we can climb the wall so we get there very very quietly from the window and grab that to guardians that are inside so that they couldn't make a sound. Then we go inside and inside and go to Zen and kill him."

Jack - "It's a splendid plan. Let's do this. Go."

Steve - "Yes, Let's go."

(Then they go very quietly there and with the help of gumboots they climb at the window and slightly remove that and go inside grabbing the two guardians there)

Steve - "Good job jack let's go inside."

Jack - "You too steve, ya let's go."

Jack - "I thought there will be traps everywhere inside the castle, but there is nothing inside there."

Steve - "No one makes the traps in open, they make it secretly that no one can imagine."

Jack - "Ok! But I can't see any trap hidden also."

Steve - "No, See there, There is a string in between that is very small that no one can see very far from their eyes."

Jack - "Ohh! But how did you get this?

Steve - "See there a stick over there flying in the sky, But it's not flying, it's on the string."

Jack - "Wow! You use your brain very sharply. Good."

Steve - "Thanks, But now get inside without tendering these strings, because these strings are combined with automatic rapid bombs, that will explode very quickly."

Jack - "Oh my god, it is now very problematic. Ok, I will try my best. Let's go."

(Then they are tendering very assiduously and completed that trap very easily)

Jack - "Yes we completed this trap but I assumed it is difficult, but it is very easy."

Steve - "No, the trap was very difficult but if anybody has stability and persistence in their body, they can pass it very easily."

Jack - "Yup, Let's go further now."

Steve - "Ya"

(Then they are going further and further completing all the traps and the moment came when they get to Zen's chamber)

Jack - "Wow!, What a room! If the problems are not there, I take a picture of this."

Steve - "Are you ready jack to go inside and fight with him."

Jack - "Ya, A little bit."

Steve - "Let's go inside"

Chapter3

The dreadful war

(Then they get inside the room but there wasn't anything inside)

Jack - "Here is nothing in the room, where is Zen.

Hello, Zen! Where are you? I know you are here. Oh! I see you are frightened of us."

Zen - "I am not hiding from you, only just trying to afraid you but you are not afraid. Hmm, you both are very afraid. But how will you fight from us."

Steve - "What! What do you mean by us."

Zen - "I mean this..."

(Then he with his army came there and the room get's invisible and the area was open from every side and very big)

Steve - "Are you ready jack, to defeat them."

Jack - "Yes but a little bit ready, but how we defeat them. They are so many. They are not in 100, not in 1000 but they are in 10000.

Steve - "So what!? You have your rock breaker sword given by that magician." You can defeat 100 in one or two hits."

Jack - "Yes, Let's go 3,2,1 Goo!."

(Then they start fighting and they both 2 are defeating their army but then after defeating all Zen's army Zen came in and they start fighting but Zen his giving them a hurting knockback and jack and steve are losing their hopes but then jack gets injured very hardly)

Steve - "Nooooo! Jack! Plss get up! get up jack we will defeat him pls get up jack"

Jack - "No I can't, he damaged me very badly, I have done my job to help you till you come here but also I am sorry that now I can't help you but you can defeat him his weakness is in his left leg toe you take the dragon sword and very hardly damage his toe."

Steve(in a crying moment)- "Yes I will ok"

Jack - "Thank you, Bye"

(Then jack died and Steve go-ahead
And then...)

Steve - "Your life is now in my hands hya!!!"

(Then he killed his leg with a dragon sword and Zen died)

(Then he get his sister Oliver and they get home with jack in his heart)

THE END

CHAPTER TWO

The Frost Walker Man

There is a small city named Venice which is a very beautiful city and the people who live there are very helpful. Suddenly in that city, a Metroid came into the plains and shacked the earth very hardly. Then a person named Pluto came there and saw something strange. Then...

Pluto - "Hey, What's this! Is it a metal box that came from the Metroid? But how is it possible! Let's open it. Oh no! It's locked. Don't worry, let's destroy it with it a stone."

(Then he takes a stone and try to destroy it)

Pluto - "Yes! I know it will destroy. Let's check it."

(Then he see something which is very weird)

Pluto - "What!! This is a pair of shoes only but who wears metal shoes and also these are shining so much. Oh, there is a paper chit also. What's this Instructions, Ok!"

(Then he read all the instructions)

Pluto - "Oh my God! These are magical shoes that have so many powers. It has infinite breathing, it can walk on water, it can also walk in the water, and also can shoot water balls. Wow, it's beautiful. Can I make a Water city in which I will be the emperor of that imperial city? Let's do that."

(Then he started taking water from everywhere from his city)

(After 6 months)

Robert- "Hey' why everybody is going to that water dam?"

The Man- "You don't know the water of our city is going somewhere."

Robert- "What! What? Are you kidding me? How can the water of our whole city can go somewhere together! It's not a living thing."

The Man- "I am not kidding you, the water from 6 months going somewhere and the animals are dying. If we don't have water we also die that's

why we are going to the dam to fill our bucket fast so that dam's water also not get lost somewhere."

(Then everybody get to the dam and took water from it but suddenly the water flew somewhere and nobody can take water properly)

(Everybody is dyeing without water)

(Then Robert gathers everybody in the meeting area and says...)

Robert- "Everybody, pls don't panic because of water loss. We will do something."

A man- "What can we do? we are not magicians that we can make water."

Robert- "Pls don't shout, don't shout. Ok nobody does anything! I will go and find water that where is it going. I will get it in 3days. In 3 days everybody has water in their home."

A Man- "Ok, we will wait for 3 days and in 3 days we drink few water and save to survive but after 3 days if you can't! We are leaving this city!"

Robert- "Ok, I am going now."

(Then he goes and try to find it)

Robert- "I have promised everyone but how will I find it? Wait! The problem starts from the day when the Metroid came here. But a Metroid can't take water on its own."

(Then his friend came there)

Robert- "Jessy! Why are you here? This slog is so dangerous. There is also a danger of life in this slog."

Jessy- "I knew it! But I am here to help you with this dangerous and confusing work. I do not afraid of anything except ghosts."

Robert- "Ok! But are you sure you can do this work?"

Jessy- "Yes! But let's do something. You have only 3 days with this half-day."

Robert- "Yes, you are right and I also thought something that we go to the place where Metroid had come because, after that destruction, water scarcity came into our city."

Jessy- "Yes you are right! But how can a Metroid take water? If this is the work of an alien! Oh my God!"

Robert- "No, aliens are nothing. It's only our misconception. Now Let's go there and investigate.

Jessy- Ok, Let's go."

(Then they go there and investigate)

Jessy- "Robert! Come here and see this! Here is a box."

Robert- "What?"

Jessy- "See this! Is it a metal box?"

Robert- "Yes, and here is a whole also like somebody tried to break it with something like stone or else. But whom?"

Jessy- "I am sure this is a work of any person of our city because only our city is here and only a human can break a lock with stone."

Robert- Yes, but whom?

Jessy- I have an idea!

Robert- What?

Jessy- "We will make a report on the people in our country and then the one who is missing is the only one who is doing this."

Robert- "Great plan, See there is a paper lying here. There is written instruction on it. Let's read it."

(Then they read the instructions and get a clue of what the thing is)

Robert- "Oh my god! That shoes are so destructive and the person wearing those shoes is making water scarcity and destruction too. We have to do something fast. Let's go and make the report."

Jessy- Yes, Let's go.

(Then at that day at night they are making reports and at next day)

(The starting of the first day)

Jessy- "Hey Robert sees this the reports say that there are 3 men and 5 women in our city who are missing, but how do we identify that who has the frost walker shoes?"

Robert- "Yes, it's difficult to find but we have to find it fast. Tell me the names!"

Jessy- "Yes, their names are Jerry, Argon, and Pluto and the women are Pinaki, Riya, Shreya, Aisha, and Trupti."

Robert- "See, the 5 women can't wear that shoes because in the instruction there was written that the shoes couldn't be worn by a woman or girl as they are made of the hard metal that is only made for men. So there are 3 suspects for us. Let's find who will be found guilty."

Jessy- "Yes, let's find. But how can we, there are 3 men so how we can be found guilty? The person wearing shoes can be anyone from the three of them!"

Robert- "Yes! You are right but we have to find it. We are left with only 2 and a half days. Can we do this?"

Jessy- "Yes we can! Don't lose your hope. I have an idea!"

Robert- "Ok I don't lose my hope but tell me that idea."

Jessy- "Yes listen, on the day when Metroid came in the plains, There is a lighthouse there which is very close to it. So we can take the CCTV camera's picture and find the guilty."

Robert- "Wow! You are brilliant Jessy. It is a great idea. Let's go there. We don't have much time."

Jessy- Thank you!

(Then they go there and then start seeing the Pictures)

Jessy- "Hey Robert see this, These are the pictures of that area and of the exact time."

Robert- "Ok let's see these pictures. No! What!?

I can't believe this!"

Jessy- "What happened!? Who is the man there in the picture and why are you shocked?"

Robert- "The name of that person is Pluto."

Jessy- "What! Pluto our friend! But why he has done this."

Robert- "Because he becomes greedy and selfish after seeing the boots and now he is making his water city and taking the entire water of our city. I got it."

Jessy- "It is a very dangerous situation, we have to go to that place where he is making his city."

Robert- "I know where he has gone, He went to the place that came before our city, The Romans land. Let's go there."

Jessy- "Wait! We don't have any weapons in our hands and he has the very powerful boots, we will defeat in one minute."

Robert- Yes you are right but what do we do then.

Jessy- "We have to take help of our scientist friend who can give us an overpowered armor which can help us defend him and he also gives us weapon which helps us to defeat him."

Robert- "Yes Let's go there."

(Then they go their where his friend is)

Robert- Is this his house?

Jessy- Yes.

Robert- "It's weird that this house is in between jungle and also made of wood but the house is awesome."

Jessy- "Are you here to see the houses made of wood? Tell me!"

Robert- Sorry, Let's go there.

Jessy- Hello George, How are you?

George- "Jessy! Robert! Why are you both here? Anything happened!"

Robert- "Yes George, Actually we both are in great danger and only you can help us in our hazardous situation."

George- "Ok, but what happened, tell me!"

Robert- Listen.

(Then Robert tells George all his story)

George- "Oh my God! So my job is to give you some equipment to fight with Pluto."

Jessy- "Yes that's why we are here."

Robert- "Pls help us!!!"

George- "Yes I can help you because I have just made some gadgets that will help you to overthrow him. Come to my lab."

Jessy- "Thank you, George, Let's go."

(Then they go to his lab and George show them some gadgets)

George- "See this armor, it will help you to defeat fire."

Robert- “George we want a suit that defeats water and storm.”

George- “Ok, I give you a multiarmour which can defend fire, water, storm, thunder, and rock also.”

Robert- “Yes, this sound’s good. Give us this armor and also show us weapons, pls.”

George- “Ok, come here, See these weapons, see this airgun which can give anybody a powerful knockback.”

Robert- “Ok It’s cool! But pls first show us the things that can defeat water and storms. But we will also take this airgun as it will help us to give Pluto and his soldiers a great knockback.”

George- “Ok, I will first show you the things to defeat water and storm. Take this freezester with you. It is one of the best things that I have ever made. It can freeze everything made of snow, water, and even it can destroy ice also.”

Jessy- “It’s great but do you have anything to destroy his shoes as he is also made of water?”

George- “Ok, for this I have one more thing, you can take this destructor but you can use it only once in a year so if you miss the shoot it will only work again after 1 year.”

Robert- “But what will it do to that shoes as that shoes cannot be destroyed without alien technology!”

George- “I know! But this destructor is also made from alien technology because I have that technology and it has only one feature that where it will be shot, the person or the whole city is destroyed very much and also take this water absorber to take water back to the city.”

Robert- “Great, Thank you so much, George. I will be thankful to you. Now we are going to defeat Pluto.”

George- “Don’t be thankful to me, we all are friends, and yes go you don’t have much time, take my bike to go faster there."

Jessy- "We will be thankful to you again for the bike also. Now we are going. Bye George."

George- "Bye, But be careful and I hope you will win."

Jessy- "Yes we will, you just don't worry."

Robert- "Let's go, Jessy, we don't have much time."

Jessy- "Yes, let's go."

(Then they were going there and on the last day, they finally reached their)

Robert- "Wow! This is amazing! He made an immense city and also it is beautiful than any city."

Jessy- "See this also, some things are made of water and some of the ice. Touch them and see it."

Robert- "Yes you are right."

Jessy- "Let's go inside, but be careful, there will be soldiers everywhere."

Robert- "Ok, let's go inside very carefully without making noise, and then with a correct time we just attack them one by one."

Jessy- Yes...

(Then they made a perfect plan and went inside)

Robert- "Jessy, you know the plan very perfectly. Now listen, we are inside the water pump machine and in the middle. I made a whole here. When I said go, we just attack them. Wear your multiarmour, take freezcter and airgun with you."

Jessy- "I have everything set up now, I am ready."

Robert- "Great! Ok, 3,2,1 Go."

(Then they start fighting and made a very bad impact on them and the soldiers are getting a knock)

(All of them died and then Pluto get the information and he came there)

Pluto- “Hey Robert and Jessy! So you both are the ones who defeated all of my armies. But why? Let me guess, You are jealous!! Yes or not.”

Robert- “No, we are not jealous! we just want you to give back the entire water you steal from the city as that was not your property. It is for the citizens who live there.”

Pluto- “And if I say no to you!”

Jessy- “Then we will kill you very desperately and make you a small physically disabled insect!!”

Pluto- Oh my god! What a confidence you have! Do you know what special thing I have through which I can do this all?

Robert- “Yes, because of these frost walker shoes. We also know all the features of these shoes. Also, we are prepared to fight with you.”

Pluto- “So what you are waiting for, let’s fight.”

(Then They started fighting)

Pluto- “You can’t defeat me because now I am not a common person, as I have an alien technology.”

Robert- “I know but we also have something.”

Pluto- “Whatever game you are playing, it won’t work. You can’t defeat me.”

Jessy- “Just shut up! You selfish boy, we are not playing a game but we also have alien technology, see this.”

Robert- “Yes, so now the fight will be equal.”

Pluto- “No, The fight will not be equal, you also know that this technology and your technology have a great difference.”

Pluto- “I am saying again, you can’t defeat me.”

Robert- “We can’t defeat you but we can remove you not from this planet but this whole galaxy.”

(Then they started fighting again and they all take their weapons in hand)

Jessy- "Robert! I am taking the shotgun out."

Robert- "Ok, I am taking the freezerter. Then take him in the middle of the air and I will shoot the destructor."

Jessy- "Ok, take the aim 1 2 3 go."

(Then she knockback him and then they go far away and Robert take aim and launch destructor)

Robert- "I launched the destructor!!! What an epic scene is this."

(Then the whole plains and pluto and his city destroyed)

Jessy- We won Robert!!! Yes! Yes! Yes!

Robert- "Yes wc won only because of you."

Jessy- "Not only me you also."

Robert- "Thank you, let's go."

(Then they went back and everyone get water back and again the city was replenished)

THE END

CHAPTER THREE

The Time Wars

There is a city named Greenville. There were three friends- George, Harry, and Lily. They are friends from kindergarten. Harry's hobby is making new inventions. Lily's hobby is to search about dinosaurs as much as she can and George's is a good shooter.

The Time Wars

George- Hello Lily

Lily- Oh! Hello George, How are you?

George- Ya, I am fine.

Lily- What are you doing here?

George- Actually Harry called me to meet in this park. What about you? What you are doing here?

Lily- Actually! Harry called me too. He is saying that he has to show me something.

George- Ok! But where is Harry? Have you seen him while coming here?

Lily- No.

George- He is late!

Lily- Ya, Nothing new. He's always late everywhere and then says that "Sorry guys for being late".

Harry- Hello Guys! Sorry for being late.

Lily- See!

(George laughing)

George- Ok! Jokes aside, tell me why you called both of us here.

Harry- Wait! Don't be in a hurry, I'm telling you. Wait. See this and tell me what's this?

George- This is just a remote!

Lily- So you just called us here to show us a remote. Is this a joke!

Harry- Wait, Wait! Just look at this remote carefully. It's not a normal remote. It has the power of time! Isn't it great?

Lily- So you mean that it's a time remote that can take us into any dimension in just a click.

George- Nice try Harry, But we are not children now that you can prank us like this.

Lily- Yes harry, I agree with George. What do you expect from us that whatever you will say we will accept it as the truth.

Harry- Guys, trust me. We can indeed go at any time.

George- Ok If it's true then prove it. Let's take us to the past dimension.

Lily- Ya prove it!

Harry- Ok! Wait, Now see...

(Then Harry clicks the button and they all travel's million's of years back and get into the past time)

Harry- See I'm not joking. We are in the past time where you can see tribes and the most important dinosaurs.

George- Wow, It's amazing! We are in past, I can't imagine this. Am I in a dream?

Lily- No, It's real. We are in past. Can we see every species of dinosaurs?

Harry- You can see everything that was in the past.

Lily- Cool!

Harry- But be aware! The dinosaurs can see you, so they can also eat you.

George- Ok, ok. Let's go forward and explore the past.

Harry- Yes, Why not. But not for a long time because I have to charge this remote. Its battery can go for only 12 hours. After 12 hours the remote will be dead and then we are unable to get back to the present time in which we are living.

Lily- Ok Ok! We understand, but how did you make this.

Harry- Actually, I traveled all the dimensions from the time machine and took the crystals that are needed to make this.

George- Wait! If you have the time machine so why did you make this remote.

Harry- I know you will ask this question. I made this because from the time machine I can just travel the specific area where I had marked it on the computer and I can mark only a few meters. (Approx.- 100m). But with this remote, I can travel the whole world with just a click.

George- Cool.

(After traveling a few hours and seeing many extinct creatures)

Harry- Guys, Let's go home. I think the remote's battery is now low. Let's go home before the remote gets dead.

Lily- Ok! No problem.

George- Ya, No problem.

(Then harry click the button and they teleport back to the Park)

George- Wait! Harry, Don't you see something weird here?

Harry- No! What do you mean? Nothing is weird here.

George- I mean the time. When we left and went to the past, the time is 2:15 and we came to the present now after many hours but the time is the same.

Harry- Oh! I forgot to tell you that whenever you leave any dimension the present time doesn't change till the next day.

George- Ok, now I understand. But this time remote is amazing. I mean who can think that we can go to the past as well as the future in just a click.

Lily- Ya! It's amazing.

Harry- Thank you, guys! Ok, now I'm leaving as I have to do my homework. Bye guys.

Lily and George- Bye!

(The next day when they all met again and harry presses the button and go into the past and after exploring THEY fight for the remote)

Harry- Why are we fighting for the remote as the main motive is to explore the past and the future.

George- Whatever happens but I have to press the remote's button.

Lily- Me too!

George- I'll press the button first.

Lily- No, I'll

Harry- No! no one will press the button except me.

(Then they all fight for the remote and the remote breaks)

Harry- No! You broke the remote!

George- Sorry Harry! I by mistake done this. Sorry, I will help you to make this again. But first, take us to the present time.

Lily- Ya me too, we both will help you to remake this after we'll get home.

Harry- The topic is not to make this again. I told you that this remote has all the three crystals of past, present, and future. And if any one of these crystals is not at its right place. The remote will not work.

Lily- So how can we get back the crystals. I mean when it broke the crystals got invisible.

Harry- If we throw the crystals, the crystals teleport themselves far away from the remote. And if we didn't get all the crystals back after some time all the dimensions will emerge. This will cause a lot of destruction. Imagine if the dinosaurs or the robots get into the present time then no one will survive. This is the time war.

George- Sorry Harry, I don't the after results.

Harry- There's no use saying sorry now. We don't have time. Let's go and find out the crystals. Everyone will go in opposite directions and find the crystals.

Lily- Wait! If we'll go alone then there are high chances of being in danger and dying.

George- Yes you are right. So we'll go together and find the crystals one by one.

Harry- Yes now it looks that we working as a team. Let's go.

George- So Harry do you have anything to get us to the crystals and take them.

Harry- No, I don't have the thing like that but I have a radar that will detect the crystals if they are in the radius of this radar.

George- Very nice, This will help us a lot.

(Then they start their journey and suddenly, after some time the radar beeps)

Harry- Wait Guys, Wait! See the radar is beeping very loudly. But where is the crystal, I can't see it?

Lily- Look at the tyrannosaurus beside the tree. He's holding it under his leg.

Harry- We have to take the crystal at any cost.

George- Have you gone mad, I mean how can we get that bloody stone out of his leg.

Lily- We have to think something.

Harry- Yes.

George- Lily you know more about dinosaurs than anyone so think how can we take the crystal. Can we tame that him?

Lily- Are you mad, it is tyrannosaurus, not a dog that we can tame him and take the stone easily.

George- So what do we do?

Lily- The only apparent weakness of T-rex was its forearms, which are not even long enough to reach its mouth. The only thing we need is something to feed him. So who will be the fodder for him?

Harry and Lily- George!!!

George- What!! But why me? Am I extra here that you're sending me there to die.

Lily- Please George, You can do this.

Harry- Yes George, You can!

George- Ok

Harry- Yes, Now we are talking. So lily you dig a hole where George will take T-rex and hide in there. And after when the T-rex will go from there I'll take the crystal and then we will leave from here for the next crystal.

Lily- Great plan harry.

Harry- Thanks.

(After getting everything done)

Harry- So George and Lily, all set.

George and Lily- Yes!

(Then George go and call T-rex to him)

George- Hey Tyranno! What's up. Come here.

Harry- Is T-rex his brother that he's calling him like that.

Lily- I don't think so.

(Then T-rex go to George to eat him but the plan works and George go into the hole and the t-rex can't catch him)

Harry- Well done George!!!

(Then harry takes the crystal)

Harry- George!! Come out, I had taken the crystal.

George- But how?

Lily- Wait! How he will come out? We didn't make a plan that how George will get out after getting inside the hole.

Harry- Yes you are right. Think something.

Lily- Idea!!!

Harry- What???

Lily- We'll attract the T-rex to us and then George will get out and we will also hide and make T-rex confuse and we'll leave.

Harry- Great, so what are we waiting for. Hurry up.

(Then harry and lily attract the t-rex towards them)

Harry- George, get out from there and go away from there. We'll meet you after getting rid of this T-rex.

George- Ok!!

(Then they make T-rex confuse and get rid of him and they all gathered again)

Harry- George! Are you okay?

George- Ya! I'm absolutely fine. Do you have the crystal?

Harry- Yes.

George- But which one is this?

Harry- This one is the past one.

Lily- Guys, Come here fast! See this.

Harry- What happened?

Lily- The worlds are emerging with the help of these teleporters.

Harry- We have to get the rest of the crystals as fast as we can. Let's Go, We don't have much time. But how do we get to the present and future?

George- Can we get to the other dimensions by these?

Lily- I think we can, Brilliant George.

Harry- Ok let's go and see where these teleporters will take us. But be careful, anything can happen to us.

Lily and George- Ok.

(Then they all step into the teleporters and then...)

George- Where are we? It doesn't seem to be the present time.

Lily- Yes you are right, it's the future. See the buses flying and robots walking.

George- Wow!! So in thc future, we'll be able to fly the vehicles.

Harry- Yes, if we can live till then.

George- What do you mean?

Harry- I mean we are in the future and here anything can happen. Imagine if the crystal is in the hands of a robot then what do we do then? The robot will shoot us and then game over!

Lily- If anything happens like this then we'll think about it. But first, can we find the crystal?

Harry- Sorry, Let's go.

Lily- Harry, do you have the radar?

Harry- Yes.

Lily- Ok, so you go first and we'll follow you.

Harry- Ok.

(Thcn thcy searched it for a long time)

George- Harry!!! Is this radar working or not as we're walking for an hour. Also, we don't have much time left now.

Harry- No it's working perfectly, I think the crystal is too far from the place where we teleported?

(Then suddenly the radar beeps)

Harry- Wait! It's beeping. But where it is?

George- See the radar is pointing towards this building. This is the main building of the future.

Lily- How do you know this?

George- I read about this on a board when we are searching for the crystal.

Harry- If it is the main building then it will be too difficult to get the crystal as there will be many guard robots and people in the building.

Lily- We have to make a plan.

Harry- Yes.

George- I have an idea!

Lily- What?

George- See, first we will scout the whole building from outside and see where the crystal is. Then we go inside the building carefully and get the crystal.

Harry- Nice plan George!!!

Lily- So, What are we waiting for! Let's go.

Harry- Ok, so George you go from the right side, and lily you go from the left and I'll go straight. After that, we will meet at the backside of this building.

Lily- Excellent plan!

George- Ya!

Harry- Thanks, Now go.

(Then they scout the whole building and meet at the backside)

Harry- So, anyone from you saw the crystal? I can't see the crystal. Lily you?

Lily- Nope.

Harry- George.

George- Yes, I saw the crystal.

Harry- Where?

George- Inside the commissioner's office, on his desk.

Lily- What, Commissioner! Is there a commissioner also?

Harry- Are you sure George?

George- Ya, I'm sure.

Harry- Ok We'll do something. Let's go inside the building and try to take it.

Lily- But there's too much risk in this.

Harry- Without taking risks, there's no means to live. Let's Go now.

(Then they all go inside the building secretly and try to reach the commissioner's room)

George- See there's the commissioner's room.

Harry- Ya, I can see it. But two robot guards are guarding the door.

Lily- So what do we do now?

Harry- George! You are a good shooter. So shoot them with your mini catapult. Do you have your mini catapult with you?

George- Yes I have, but if I missed it?

Harry- There's no question of missing.

Lily- George, Be calm and carefully hit it.

George- Ok.

(Then he hits both of them and the robots get bad)

Harry- Yes!!!

Lily- I know! You can do this George.

George- Thanks. Now go and take the crystal.

Lily- Which one's this?

Harry- This is the present one. Now only the future one is left.

George- Yes, we can do it. If it will be in the present time. It will be too much easy for us to take it.

Harry- No, because the future one is not a simple crystal. The future crystal is the difficult one to get because it is very fast no one can take it very easily.

Lily- But we will try to take it.

George- Yes, we'll try our best. If we can take the crystals from dinosaurs and robots then that will also not be a big deal.

Harry- Thanks for encouraging.

Lily- Let's go now.

(Then they come outside of the building and see that...)

Lily- Boys, can you see this?

Harry- Yes, these crystals are emerging and becoming larger and larger. We have to take the crystal fast or everyone will be teleported to another dimension if they see these teleporters.

George- But how do we find out, which teleporter teleports us to the present time?

Harry- We have to search for it. We have to go through each of the teleporters and see that which one is the present one.

George- Ok.

(Then they go through each portal, but they can't find the present one)

Lily- Where is that bloody portal?

Harry- We don't have to give up, Let's go through that portal behind the bushes.

(Then they go through that portal and teleports to the present time)

Lily- Is this the present time?

Harry- Yes, it's the present one only.

George- We find it. Yes.

Harry- Let's go and find out that crystal and fix everything back.

Lily- Put that radar on.

Harry- Yes.

(Then they search for the crystal and after some time the radar beeps)

Harry- Guys, it's beeping.

Lily- Harry! Is this your house?

Harry- Yes, It's my house. So the crystal is in my house.

George- So what are you waiting for? Let's go.

(Then they search for the crystal in the house but they didn't get it)

George- Finding crystals in ancient time and future time is too easy than finding in this house.

Harry- Guys, look upon the shelf of the kitchen.

Can you see something shiny there?

George- Yes, I can see that crystal!!! Let's take it.

(Then George tries to take it but the crystal runs away from him)

Harry- See I told you, it's very fast.

(Then they try too much to catch it but can't and then...)

Harry- See we will try to catch it from different sides. Lily, you go from right, and George from left, and I'll stand here. George, you step forward and try to catch it.

(Then they all catch it when they work as a team)

Harry- Yes we catch it.

George- Yes!!!

Harry- Now we can fix cverything.

Lily- Harry! Do it fast see all the teleporters are emerging now and making a big one.

Harry- Yes I'm doing it.

Lily- Fast!!!

Harry- Done!

(Then after a few seconds, the teleporters disappear)

Harry- Yes, now everything is normal.

George- Harry, now throw it far away.

Harry- No if by mistake someone stepped on it then this will happen again. I will put it in my locker carefully so that nobody except me can take it.

George- Ok now I'm going home to take some rest.

Lily- Ya me too.

Harry- Me too guys. Bye!

(Then they all lived happily)

The End

CHAPTER FOUR

The Detective Engineer

A long time back, In 9th CE There was a village named Shitalpur. The whole village was very attractive and beautiful. The people who lived there were very helpful and educated. In that village, there lived a person named Bhimraj who was the king of the village and was very selfish and greedy but the people who lived there don't know this, They see him like he is a god gift for them. After some time when the king has not a lot of money to spend on his new dresses, his food. He was very upset so he thought something and did that and he became successful in it. And then he again became rich but this time he became more rich day by day. At that time in the village, a person came out of his shelter and shouted so much that "ohhhh no my money was stolen, there was a thief inside our village my entire money was stolen" and cried so much then he went to their king and tell him that his money was stolen. So the king said he see his case and work on it. After that next day again someone's money was stolen. And then day by day everybody's money was stolen and the king only says to them that he will work on it but he doesn't. but at next day a person who was an engineer came and also see him as a detective. He went into the village and he saw in the village someone crying and asked him why he was crying so he tell him that don't you know that from a week one by one everybody's money was stolen. So he thinks that it's strange that day by day everybody's money was stolen. So he told everybody that they don't panic he does something so he noticed some days that from where and when the money was stolen so he got that the money was stolen always at night and the person did not come from the gate he climbs the roof and came into the house slowly. Then he realized that the thief was only stealing the things from villagers, not from the king why? So he, at that night went to the king's palace secretly and checked there and he saw that the whole money of the entire village was at the king's palace. So the next day he tells everybody about it but no one trusts him and said to him that their king was very good. Nobody understands him so he tells them that he will take the very old and senior man of the village so at that night he takes the senior villager with him secretly and then he told him to see that the whole money was with the king. So the next day everybody came to the king's palace and said to him that you are the one who stolen my money so the king said I'm not that who stolen my money so the detective said everybody to go into the king's money room they went there and see that he was stealing their money so everybody was very angry and said that the king will die so everybody makes him hang on and made the detective their king but the engineer detective said that the village is of the villagers, not anybody else and gone from there. After that, the engineer was in everybody's heart.

CHAPTER FIVE

The Self Made Girl

A long time back in the year 1986, There was a girl named Laxmi who was 18 years above and was very beautiful. She was a well-mannered and educated girl. Like everybody, She also has many dreams (to be a teacher, to open a coaching center, and many more), but she doesn't know that she was going to live a married life. Her parents are deciding to make her a married person. When she knew that she tried so much to make them understand that she does not want to get married now and wanted to study more but they don't hear anything and made her a bride. Now she was living the married life in which every time she does households and households. She doesn't get time for herself. After a few months, she became a mother, She has a cute and little girl and she named her chiki. Everyone was happy but chiki's mother was worried about her life that does she also has to live a married and do household. Then her mother decided that she also not live a married life although she make her dreams fulfill and after that she by own decision when to live a married life. Then she teaches chiki lessons of life and tells to be a self-made girl and never lose her strength. Then chiki understood everything and promised her mother that she will become a good and a big person. After promising this she studied very much done graduation and done LLB.

And today, She was a very famous lawyer and has won many cases.

Here's the list of cases she has won and lost

TOTAL CASES WON CASES LOST CASES

137 128 09

9 798885 690683

Printed by Libri Plureos GmbH in Hamburg,
Germany